# A Day with No Internet!

Story by Jill McDougall

Illustrations by Omar Aranda

## Contents

# Chapter 1

## Annabel's Game

Annabel was playing a game
on her tablet.

"I have to feed a cute baby seal,"
she told Mum.

Annabel tapped on her tablet.
**Tap! Tap!**

"I must find some fish for my seal!"
she said.

Mum gave Annabel a quick smile.
She was working on her laptop
and she was too busy to talk.

At last, Annabel found some fish
to feed her seal.
She tapped on her tablet
to scoop up the fish.

But the game had stopped working!

Annabel was upset.
"Mum!" she cried. "I can't feed my baby seal!"

Mum was tapping the keys on her laptop.
"My laptop is getting slower!" she said,
in a cross voice.

# Chapter 2

## No Wi-Fi!

Just then, Annabel's brother Hayden came into the room.

"I can't do my school work!" he cried. "I can't connect to the internet!"

Annabel jumped up.
"It must be the Wi-Fi," she said.

Annabel looked at the little black box
beside the sofa.
The green light on the front of the box was not on.

The Wi-Fi had stopped working!

"What are we going to do without any internet?" asked Hayden.

"My pet seal will be hungry!" cried Annabel.

This made Hayden laugh.

"It's not funny, Hayden!" shouted Annabel. And she went to her bedroom, shutting the door behind her.

# Chapter 3

## Fun Family Games

Annabel sat on her bed, feeling cross.
It was hard to have fun without the internet!

After a while, Annabel looked at some books beside her bed.
One book was called *Fun Family Games*.

"Hmm," said Annabel to herself.
"Maybe we could all play a game."

She took the book to show Mum and Hayden.

FUN
FAMILY
GAMES

Hayden found a game in the book called “Toss the Toy”.

“Let’s play this game,” he said.

Soon, Mum, Hayden and Annabel were playing the game in the backyard.

Annabel was the first player.
She had to turn around three times,
then toss a toy giraffe into a basket.

It was hard to get the giraffe in the basket
after turning around and around!

Everyone was laughing!

## Chapter 4

# Dad Has a Turn

When Dad came home,
he was surprised to see the family
playing together.

"Let me have a turn," said Dad, smiling.

Dad turned around three times
and tried to toss the giraffe into the basket.

It dropped into the wheelbarrow!

Hayden laughed so hard,
he made a funny noise like a horse.
This made everyone laugh even more!

Soon the internet came back on,
but everyone wanted to keep playing games.

Annabel said, "I'm glad the Wi-Fi stopped working.
I think we should have a 'No Internet Day'
every week!"

And that's just what they did.